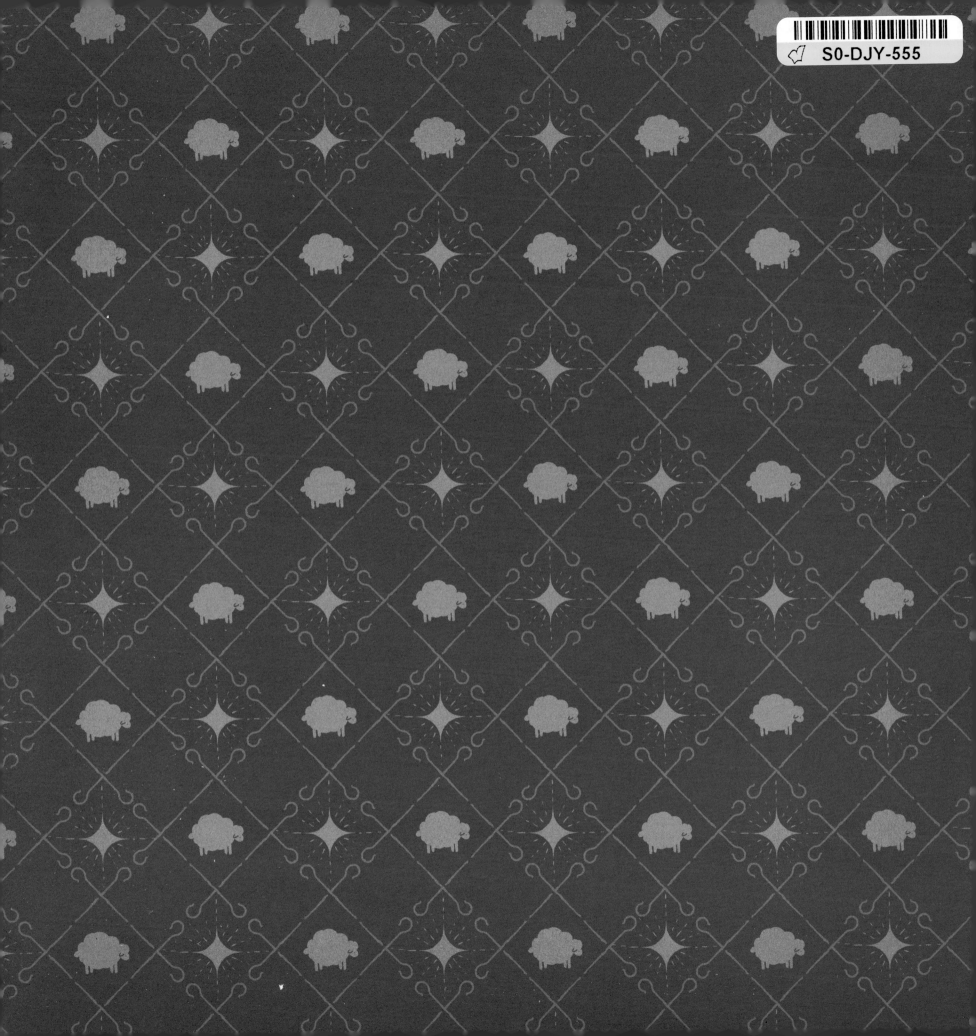

This season is full of exciting things—
cookies and lights, and gifts Christmas brings!

There are tales of enchantment and sugar plum fairies
and beautiful music and red holly berries.

But the most wonderful thing—did you know?
Is the MIRACLE that happened a long time ago!

To tell you this story, a Shepherd was sent.
He wants you to know what Christmas
REALLY meant!

Before telling the secret of Christmas' fame,
this tiny young Shepherd must have a NAME!

Call him Rudy or Alan or Zipadee-Flick!
Whatever his name, please choose one quick!

Once you have named him, your Shepherd will start
on a magical journey close to his heart.

He travels by night when everyone's asleep,
so shut those eyes tight, and be sure to not peek!

When you wake in the morning, wherever you find him,
don't disturb him or move him, just follow behind him.

He's off on a quest, and he wants you there, too,
to join in his journey, to seek what is True.

At the end of this trip, he wants you to find
the biggest treasure of Christmastime!

This treasure hunt began long ago, one dark night,
when stars filled the sky with bright Christmas light.

Your Shepherd boy was watching his sheep
when quietly, he started to weep.

Tears filled his eyes and he sniffled his nose,
for he wished he could be a young prince with fine clothes.

Then he'd have friends and mountains of toys,
and he wanted those things, like all shepherd boys.

He looked up at the stars, feeling quite small
and began to wonder, "Am I special at all?"

He breathed out a sigh—"Does anyone care?"
Then all of a sudden . . . someone was there!

In a great flash of light an angel appeared—
the most beautiful creature that hovered and neared!

He lit the whole sky and the glow was so bright—
you'd think it was day, not late, late at night!

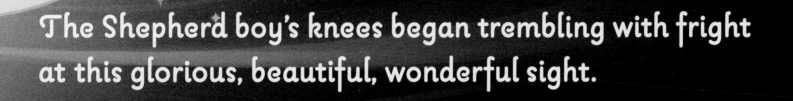

The Shepherd boy's knees began trembling with fright
at this glorious, beautiful, wonderful sight.

But when he looked into the angel's kind eyes,
the angel spoke gently, with words sweet and wise . . .

"It is the very first Christmas! And soon to unfold,
is the story of treasure worth far more than gold.

In the small town of Bethlehem, moments ago
a baby was born with an angelic glow.

His name is called Jesus—he's the promised one.
We've been waiting for Him—God's very own Son!

Tonight is the night when his story begins,
when he's grown he will save all the world from its sins.

He's the king of all kings, though now he's just small.
Yes, this little baby's the BEST treasure of all!

Then the angel drew close and whispered into his ear
the important mission he needed to hear.

"For exciting adventures, momentous and huge,
God chooses the little people just like YOU!"

Jesus came to be big for those who are small
and to love those who think they don't matter at all.

Your job, little Shepherd, is so very special.
This assignment is one that must be successful!

You will help children find treasure each Christmas
and lead them to love they'll find only in Jesus."

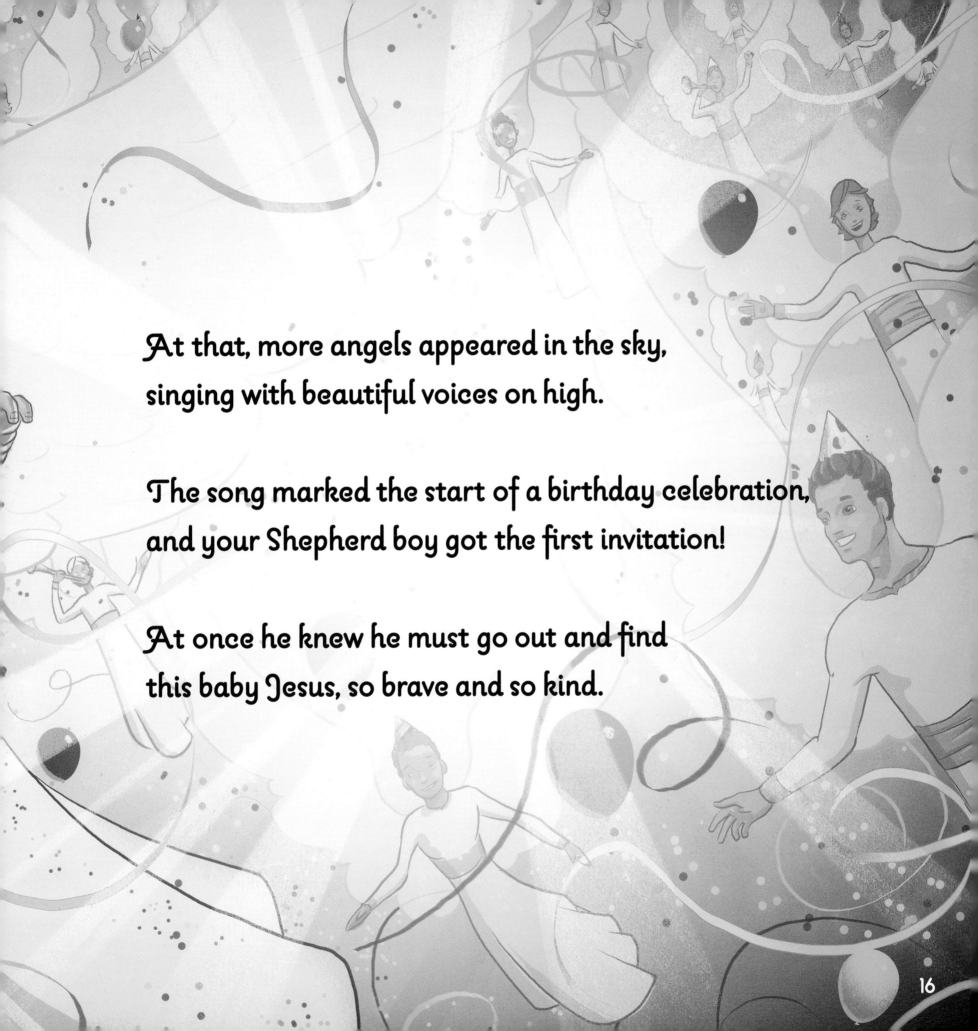

At that, more angels appeared in the sky,
singing with beautiful voices on high.

The song marked the start of a birthday celebration,
and your Shepherd boy got the first invitation!

At once he knew he must go out and find
this baby Jesus, so brave and so kind.

Many years have now passed since that wonderful night,
when the angels appeared and made the sky bright,

but the Shepherd boy always remembers his call
to visit each year and share his quest with us all.

So now GO with your Shepherd to find this treasure,
this Jesus whose love is great without measure!

That time has come NOW! This moment! This minute!
The tale has begun . . . and this time YOU'RE in it!

Starting tomorrow, each day when you rise,
look for your Shepherd—he's seeking the prize!

Follow the steps of his journey each day—
as he searches for Jesus, he'll show you the way!

Where will you look? Search high and search low!
When you finally find him, you are sure to know!

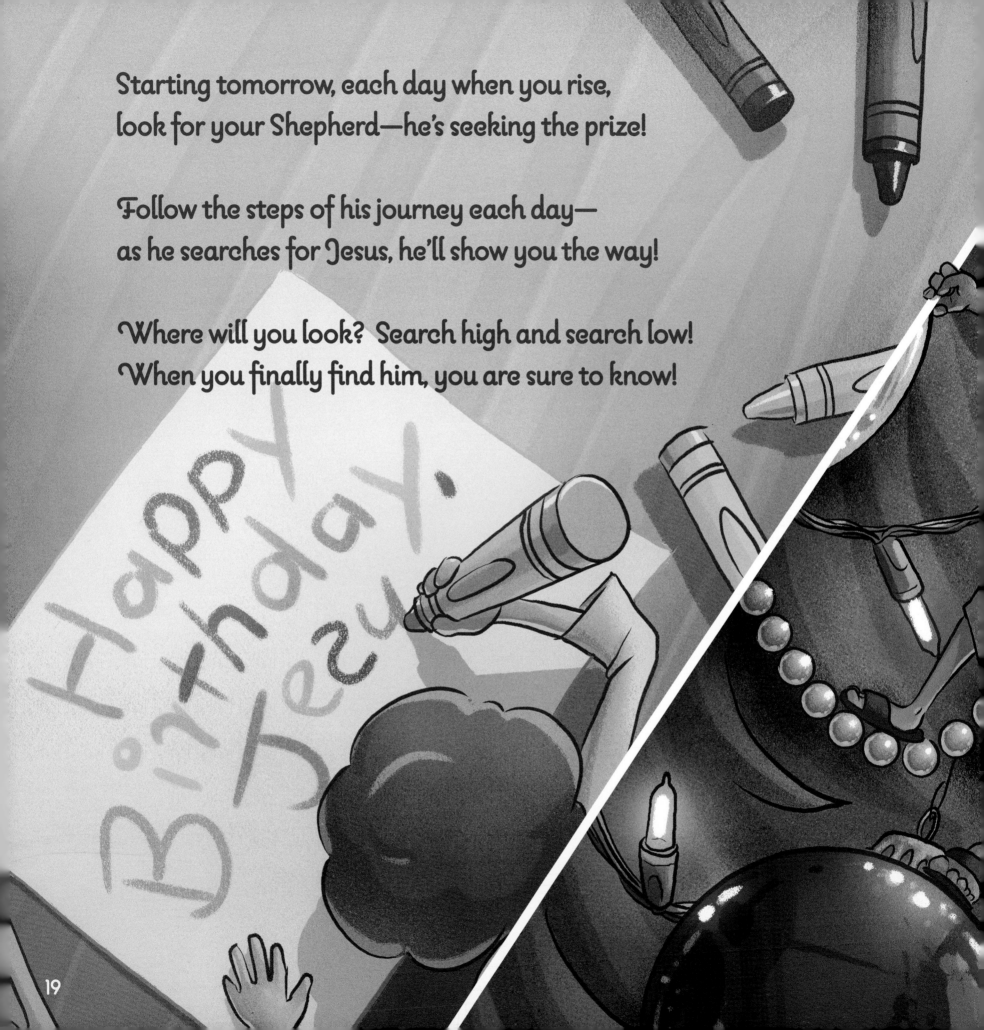

The baby will be
on a soft bed of hay . . .

just as he was on that first Christmas day!

Don't ever stop searching, when Christmas is done,
for Jesus, the Savior, the Holy One.

In all that you say and in all that you do,
try to find Jesus, and he will find you!

When your heart becomes sad and you're feeling so low,
when you don't feel important, Jesus wants you to know

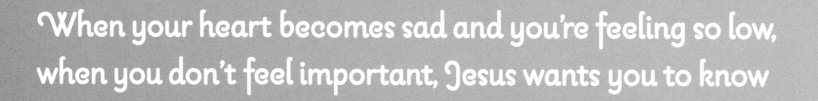

that he too was once small but is now King of Kings—
in him, you are made for VERY big things!

Hi There!

It's me—Your Shepherd friend! Thanks for taking this exciting journey with me to find Jesus. I thought it might help if I told you a little more about baby Jesus and why he's so special!

You see, God (who made the sky and the animals and you and me) saw that we were lost like little sheep without a Shepherd. We needed help to find our way back home to him.

Why were we lost? We were lost because of sin. Have you ever done something bad that made your mommy or daddy mad or sad? Things like not telling the truth or not listening to your parents or not sharing are all sins that hurt God's heart. God is your Father in Heaven. He loves you so much and has a great plan for you, but sin gets in the way and keeps you far from him.

That's why God planned a special rescue mission to bring us close to him again! He sent his very own son Jesus to be born into our world on Christmas. Yes, God loved the world so much that he gave his only Son, so that everyone who believes in him would not be lost anymore and could live with him in heaven one day (John 3:16, paraphrase).

The Bible says that if you believe that Jesus came to bring us close to God again, you become part of God's family, and Jesus will come and be your friend forever, too! Do YOU believe this? If you do, you can tell Jesus right now!

Dear Jesus,

I know that sometimes I don't always do the right things. I know that my sins are wrong and that they hurt your heart, but I believe that, because you love me so much, you came to save me from my sins! Thank you! Please forgive me, come into my heart, and be my friend forever! Amen.

Now your own special journey with Jesus has begun! He wants you to read and learn the Bible so you can know him better. You can talk to him when you pray and tell him about your day!

Jesus says, "When you search for me with all your heart, you will find me" (Jeremiah 29:13, ERV). Don't ever stop searching for Jesus, no matter what! Merry Christmas!

Love,

your
shepherd

Bible Verse Treasure Hunt!

Each set of pages in your book has a hidden Bible verse! The Bible tells us to, "Look for wisdom like silver. Search for it like hidden treasure" (1 John 2:4, ERV). Go and find where each verse in the book is hidden and discover what it says!

Verse Key:

Pages 1-2:
"Then I will give you shepherds who are dear to my heart. Their knowledge and understanding will help them lead you." - Jeremiah 3:15 (NIRV)

Pages 3-4:
"A good name is worth more than silver or gold." - Proverbs 22:1 (ERV)

Pages 5-6:
"But seek first his kingdom and his righteousness, and all these things will be given to you as well." - Matthew 6:33 (NIV)

Pages 7-8:
"The Lord does not look at the things people look at. People look at the outward appearance but the Lord looks at the heart." - 1 Samuel 16:7 (NIV)

Pages 9-10:
"That night, some shepherds were out in the fields near Bethlehem watching their sheep. An angel of the Lord appeared to them, and the glory of the Lord was shining around them. The shepherds were very afraid. The angel said to them, "Don't be afraid. I have some very good news for you—news that will make everyone happy." - Luke 2: 8-10 (ERV)

Pages 11-12:
"God loved the world SO much that he sent Jesus, his only son, so that anyone who believes in him will not die but will live forever in heaven as part of God's family! God didn't send Jesus into the world to punish people but to rescue them from their sins and bring them close to God again!" - John 3:16-17 (paraphrase)

Pages 13-14:

"But Jesus called the children to him and said, "Let the little children come to me, and do not hinder them, for the kingdom of God belongs to such as these."" - Luke 18:16 (NIV)

Pages 15-16:

"Then a huge army of angels from heaven joined the first angel, and they were all praising God, saying, 'Praise God in heaven, and on earth let there be peace to the people who please him.' The angels left the shepherds and went back to heaven. The shepherds said to each other, 'Let's go to Bethlehem and see this great event the Lord has told us about.' So they went running and found Mary and Joseph. And there was the baby, lying in the manger. When they saw the baby, they told what the angels said about this child. Everyone was surprised when they heard what the shepherds told them. Mary continued to think about these things, trying to understand them. The shepherds went back to their sheep, praising God and thanking him for everything they had seen and heard. It was just as the angel had told them."
- Luke 2:13-20 (ERV)

Pages 17-18:

"I love those who love me; and those who seek me with all their heart will find me." - Proverbs 8:17 (paraphrase)

Pages 19-20:

"Let the hearts of those who seek the Lord rejoice. Look to the Lord and his strength; seek his face always."
- 1 Chronicles 16:10-11 (NIV)

Pages 21-22:

"You will seek me and find me when you seek me with all your heart." - Jeremiah 29:13 (NIV)

Pages 23-24:

"In all your ways acknowledge him and he will make your paths straight." - Proverbs 3:6 (NIV)

Pages 25-26:

"God says, 'I have great plans for you! I don't want to hurt you. I plan to give you hope and a wonderful future. When you call on my name and come to me and pray to me, I will listen to you. You will search for me, and when you search for me with all your heart, you will find me. I will let you find me.'" - Jeremiah 29: 11-13 (paraphrase)

This is for my sweet Charlotte and little Maverick! My greatest prayer is that you come to love the Lord with all your heart, all your soul and all your mind! This book would not have been possible without the support of Brett, my husband and my very best friend! I love you! You and our amazing Sleepingbaby.com team have worked so hard to take things off of my plate so I could focus on this book. I am so thankful that God pulled on my heart until I obeyed the call to write it. To HIM be the glory . . . GREAT things He has done!

"Jesus said, 'Let the little children come to me, and do not hinder them,
for the kingdom of heaven belongs to such as these.'"
–Matthew 19:14 (NIV)

A HUGE thanks to my incredibly talented Editors and FRIENDS:
Meg Shideler
Julie Rhodes
Carolyn Lee
Jenny Lindquist

Mike Marshall: Your beautiful artwork has brought this book to life!! THANK YOU!

Our **CHRIST**mas tradition began for the

Byington

family

on _December_, 20_17_

when we named our Shepherd

Red
.

Now we are off on our treasure

quest to find Jesus!

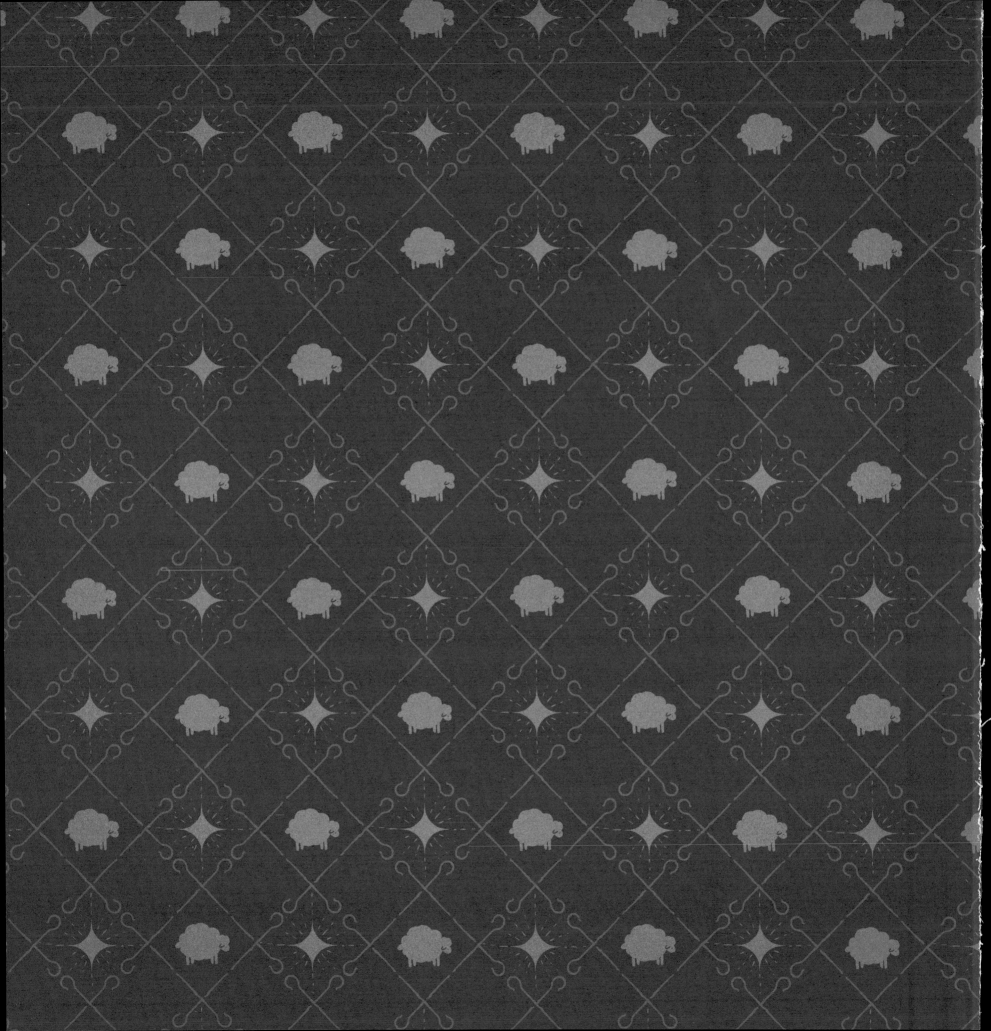